# MONSTER CHEFS

## BRIAN & LIAM ANDERSON

A NEAL PORTER BOOK
ROARING BROOK PRESS
NEW YORK

Copyright © 2014 by Brian Anderson
A Neal Porter Book
Published by Roaring Brook Press
Roaring Brook Press is a division of Holtzbrinck Publishing Holdings Limited Partnership
175 Fifth Avenue, New York, New York 10010
mackids.com

Library of Congress Cataloging-in-Publication Data

Anderson, Brian 1974–
    Monster chefs / Brian and Liam Anderson. — First edition.
        pages cm
    "A Neal Porter Book."
    Summary: Tired of eating only eyeballs and ketchup, a horrible king
sends his four monster chefs out to find something different for him to
eat, with surprising results.
    ISBN 978-1-59643-808-8 (hardcover : alk. paper)
[1. Cooks—Fiction. 2. Monsters—Fiction. 3. Diet—Fiction. 4. Kings,
queens, rulers, etc.—Fiction. 5. Humorous stories.] I. Anderson, Liam
D. II. Title.
    PZ7.A5228Mon 2014
    [E]—dc23
                                                            2012046930

Roaring Brook Press books may be purchased for business or promotional use.
For information on bulk purchases please contact Macmillan Corporate and Premium Sales Department
at (800) 221-7945 x5442 or by email at specialmarkets@macmillan.com.

First edition 2014
Book design by Jennifer Browne and Roberta Pressel
Printed in China by Toppan Leefung Printing Ltd., Dongguan City, Guangdong Province

1   3   5   7   9   10   8   6   4   2

For Emily and Thomas
Liam would also like to thank his mom.
And a monstrous thank you to Rosemary, Neal, and Jennifer.

# "CHEFS!"

The monster king bellowed for his chefs. The king happened to be a horribly horrible monster, which made him an excellent king.

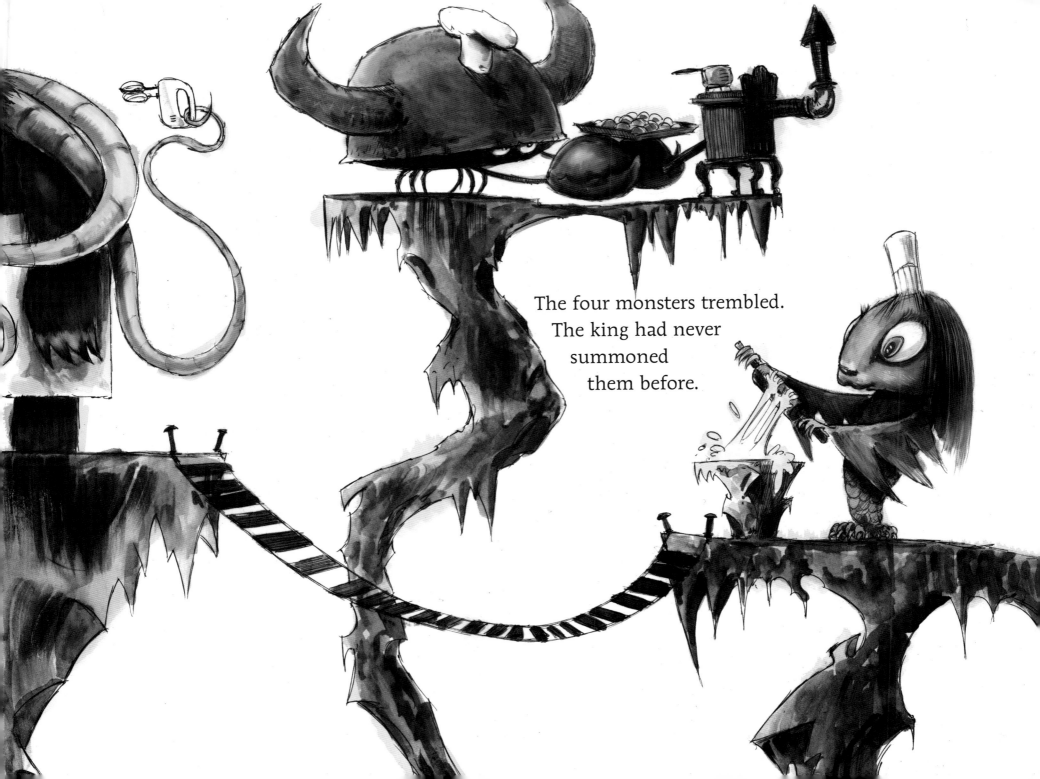

The four monsters trembled.
The king had never
summoned
them before.

"I am tired of eating only eyeballs and ketchup," roared the king. "Find me something new to eat or you will find yourselves on my menu!"

Fur flew and hats fell.

You see, monsters, as far back as any monster could remember, only ever ate eyeballs and ketchup.

The chefs trudged away from the castle in different directions.

 The first chef blundered north,  through prickly forests and rolling mountains,

until there was only snow and ice as far as a monster could see. Which is quite far indeed.

"I have traveled as far as I can go," he wailed. "And I have not found one new thing for my king to eat."

The chef slogged back toward the castle, his tentacled head slumped low. Just then he glimpsed a tiny, furry creature hopping through the snow. He snatched it up and sniffed it with his shriveled snout.

"You will make a tasty dish for my king!" said the monster, smiling a tooth-filled monster smile.

"Obviously your king has never eaten rabbit before," said the rabbit.

The monster shook his tentacled head. "No, he only eats eyeballs and ketchup."

"Well," said the rabbit, looking as serious as a rabbit could, "your king will be awfully upset with you if you serve me up for dinner."

"Why?" asked the monster.

"Look around you," said the rabbit.

The monster did look around and saw more rabbits than a monster could count, springing through the deep snow.

"If you eat a rabbit, you turn into a rabbit. That is why there are so many of us."

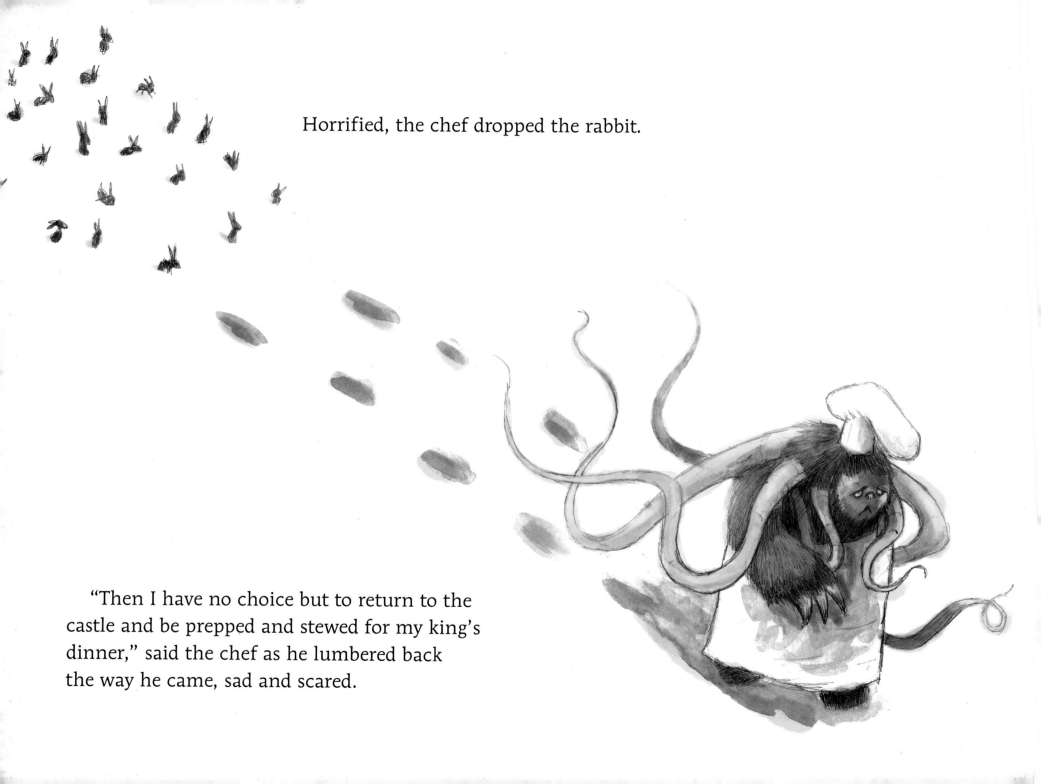

Horrified, the chef dropped the rabbit.

"Then I have no choice but to return to the
castle and be prepped and stewed for my king's
dinner," said the chef as he lumbered back
the way he came, sad and scared.

The second monster chef stomped off southward
till her claw-tipped foot touched the ocean.

She saw water as far as a monster could see,
and that, as you know, is far indeed.

"I have walked as far as I can walk and
have found not a single thing for my king
to eat," she said.

As she watched her tears fall into the ocean, something scaly swam between her mossy toes. She scooped it up.

"Oh, I am so happy to have caught you," she said. "My king will find you scrumptious!"

Now the fish was from a school so it was quite smart.

"Your king would be cross with you if you served me for his supper," it said.

"And why is that?" asked the monster.

"Everyone knows that if you eat a fish you turn into one," said the fish. "That is why the ocean is crammed full of fish."

So the chef dropped the fish back
into the ocean and shuffled
back the way she came.

Now the third monster chef skittered into the west,
over cloud-topped mountains and carved valleys,
until he came to a sandy place where the sand
spread out as far as a monster could see.
And that is far indeed.

"I have failed to find a new delectable delight
for my king to eat," said the chef.
And as he slunk back to the east, something
slithered between his crabby legs.

"Oh, glorious day," cried the monster chef. "My king will find you exceptionally succulent!"

"Obviously your king hasssss never eaten a ssssssnake before," said the snake, coiling about the monster's claw.

"What do you mean by that?" he asked.

"Look around you," said the snake. "When you eat a sssssnake you turn to sssssand."
The monster gazed around at the shimmering sand.

"That would make my king angry," he said. "He loathes sand. Thank you for saving my king, but now I must return home so I can be served up for his dinner."

He placed the snake down on the sand and slunk off toward the castle.

The three monster chefs huddled together in the king's court awaiting their punishment. The king, spit seething from his massive mouth, glared down at them.

"Not one of you has found something new and tasty for me to eat," roared the king, spattering the chefs with globs of green drool. "I shall now eat all three of you!"

The king paused, raising his single hedge-sized eyebrow.

"I thought there were four of you."

As the king proceeded to count the chefs
with his taloned fingers, the fourth chef
bounded into the court.

"And I suppose you have also failed to bring something savory to eat," said the king. "Please slather yourselves in ketchup, as I am outrageously hungry and wish to devour the four of you right now!"

"Wait, your hideousness," said the fourth chef. "I did find something new for you to eat."

The king squinted his one eye at the chef. "Show it to me."

The fourth monster chef gingerly lifted his chef's hat.

The others gasped at what stood atop the chef's furry head.

"Well, that looks awful," said the king. "It is too small, too scrawny, and smells of soap."

The other three monsters sighed and resumed pouring ketchup over their heads.

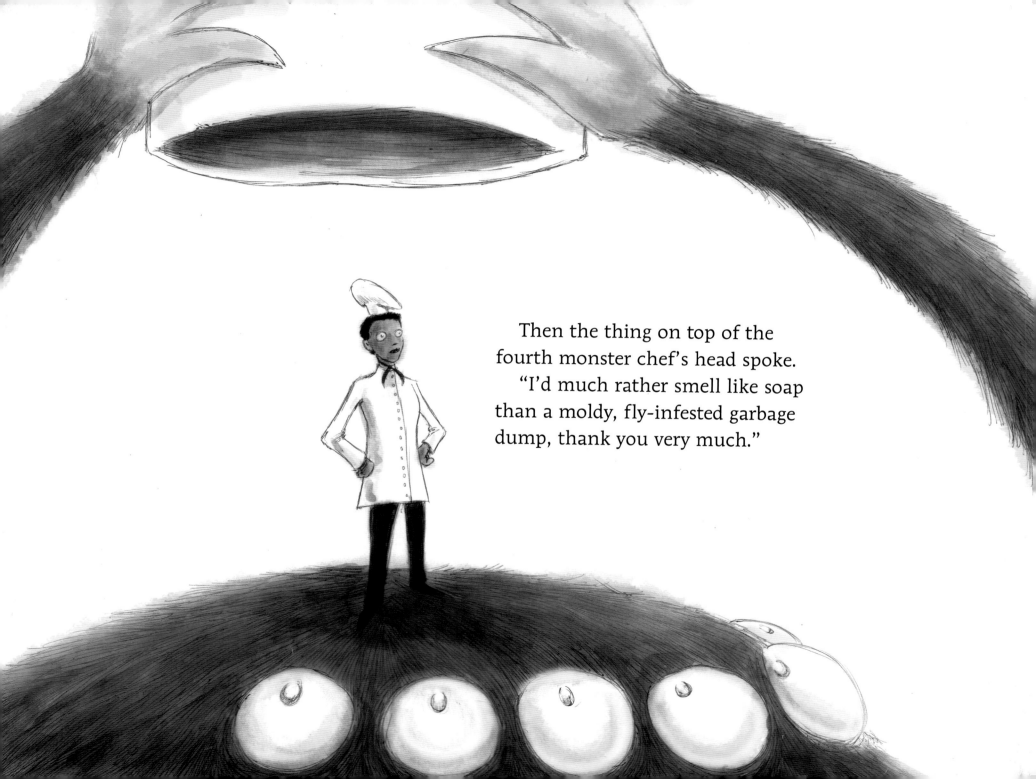

Then the thing on top of the fourth monster chef's head spoke.
"I'd much rather smell like soap than a moldy, fly-infested garbage dump, thank you very much."

"Oh, she's not for eating," said the fourth monster chef. "She's a chef!"

The monster king loomed over the tiny thing. "I shall eat you anyway just for being so rude!"

The pastry chef produced a tiny cardboard box from her jacket.

Standing on tiptoes, she held the contents of the box up to the monster king.

"A pastry chef," said the young woman, smiling proudly up at the king of monsters.

She untied the red string.

The king carefully took it between the tips of his talons.

He sniffed it.

He growled at it, and finally . . .

. . . he licked it.

The king popped it into his maw

and did something no monster had ever done.

He danced. He sang. He roared with delight.
And from that day onward, monsters throughout the world only feasted on cupcakes.

Cupcakes decorated with eyeballs, of course.

# EYEBALL CUPCAKES

WARNING: Do *not* track down a monster on your own and ask for an eyeball. This is horribly dangerous. Instead, ask a grown-up to help you follow the recipe on this page.

## Cupcake Recipe
Yield: 20 cupcakes

Ingredients:
$1\frac{1}{2}$ cups flour
1 cup sugar
1 teaspoon baking soda
1 teaspoon salt
$\frac{1}{2}$ cup cocoa powder
1 cup water
$\frac{1}{2}$ cup vegetable oil
1 teaspoon vinegar

Directions:
1. Put all of the ingredients in a large bowl and mix with a mixer or wooden spoon. Batter should be brown and smooth, free of lumps.
2. Pour into a lined cupcake tin until each cup is about three-quarters full.
3. Bake at 350 F for 25 minutes.

## Frosting Recipe

Ingredients:
2 cups powdered sugar
2 tablespoons butter or margarine, softened
2 tablespoons milk
$\frac{1}{2}$ teaspoon vanilla extract

Directions:
1. Combine ingredients in a mixer on medium speed until smooth and fluffy.

## For the Eyeballs

Now obtain a variety of Monster Eyeball Simulator Supplies (M.E.S.S.). For the cupcake drawing on this page I used Lifesaver Gummies for the iris, M&Ms for the pupil, and red cake decorating gel for the veins.